A Note from the Author

When I was at school, I was always looking for adventure. So was my friend, Carole. This book is for her.

Close to our school there was a very old house. No one lived there, so one day we made up our minds to look round the garden, which was full of weeds. We found some steps. At the bottom of them was a door, which wasn't locked, but it was too dark inside to see anything.

We came back the next day with a torch, and found the vault that you read about in the story. It was very creepy in there, because it was under the ground and there was no noise. So when I wanted to write a scary story, that was the place that came into my mind ...

For Carole, alias Wurdle

Contents

Chapter 1
The Impossible Pot

Far away, the thunder growled like a mad dog. Melanie looked up. The sky had gone very dark, and a moment later she felt the first drop of rain. She was standing at the top of Hangman's Hill, at the entrance to a little museum. She could see the building at the end of a twisting path, so she made a run for it. The door was old, and very heavy. It seemed to be stuck, but in the end it creaked open, and she slipped inside.

It was even darker in there than it had been outside, and she could hear shuffling foot-steps. She thought she saw a distant flash of a dark green uniform, and white hair. Then a light flickered on. After that the foot-steps went away again, and she was alone once more.

So why could she hear tapping right beside her?

There really was no one in sight. The noise was coming from *inside* a display cabinet. She peered through the glass and saw a large Greek vase. On it were painted a tree, a dog and a man. *And the figures were moving.*

Melanie rubbed her eyes. The man seemed to be trapped on the surface of the vase. It was as if he was behind a pane of glass, and he was tapping it to test its thickness. The dog was big and white and powerful, a bit like a pointer. Then Melanie saw that the man was digging away at a hair-line crack with a knife.

Suddenly the dog froze, and the man turned to look. Something dark slid round the side of the vase. The dog sank to his belly, and the man backed away until he was up against the tree. Black shapes were swirling into view, and the man had a look of terror on his face. Everything was happening in total silence.

Melanie became aware that she was hardly breathing. The figures in front of her were more real than any she had ever seen in a painting. Her mouth had gone very dry. And then the man looked up, and saw her through the crack.

His mouth dropped open and he looked amazed. Then his expression changed, and he signalled in panic for her to break the vase. When she didn't respond he got down onto his knees and placed his fore-head on the ground, facing towards her. He was begging her, in silence, and it was as clear as it would have been 3,000 years earlier.

Melanie lifted the lid of the display case. Three women slid into view, their black clothing floating out behind them like smoke. They had snakes twisted round their arms, whips in their hands, and torches that blazed and spat sparks. A sudden gale shook the branches of the tree.

The man looked trapped. And then, just as though someone somewhere had turned up the volume, Melanie began to hear voices. The language was strange but she understood the sense. Her mind slipped into a new gear and she found the words.

"Seize him," hissed one of the women, her hands like claws.

"Hold him."

"He is ours by law."

"In the name of Zeus!" the man cried out to Melanie. "Break the vase!"

Melanie leant into the case, leant in so far that she felt the wooden frame cut into her. She picked up the pot. It felt smooth and cold, like stone, but it quickly warmed through and then it began to feel like skin, not clay. She shut her eyes and smashed the pot against the edge of the display case, and it broke with a dull clunk.

Melanie blinked, and looked at what she'd done. The vase was worth a lot of money, and her fingerprints would be all over it. Maybe it could be mended.

She turned over the pieces, one by one. She saw that the pot had broken down the hair-line crack. The paint was different there, as though it had been broken and mended many times. On the first bit she could see the tree. On the second one she could see the man's body, lying on the ground. His head would be on the third fragment. She picked it up and dropped it again, the way she would have done if she'd picked up a plum and found it crawling with maggots. The women were lying in a heap on the other side, tangled together. One of them raised her head and looked right at her. There was no doubt at all that she saw her. The man's head was lying at the woman's feet. For one awful moment Melanie thought that she herself had cut off the man's head by breaking the vase ... then she saw a knife, lying beside him. She was suddenly quite sure that the three women had killed him.

"Melanie Dunn ..." The voice was the wind echoing through an empty building.

"We claim you, Melanie Dunn," hissed the second woman. "It is the law."

"We are the Kindly Ones," breathed the third.

They didn't look very kind. Melanie slammed the display case shut, turned, and ran. When she reached the main door something brushed against her leg. She felt dizzy, and she put out a hand to steady herself. The door suddenly gave and swung open. She was outside in the sun-light, and there was a large white dog beside her. His tail waved back and forth, and he licked her on the hand. *It's the dog from the vase*, thought Melanie, jerking her arm away as though he'd bitten her. *But that's just not possible.*

And although he seemed friendly, she had never been so scared in her life.

Chapter 2
The Dog from Nowhere

The dog from the vase was a big dog, a hunting dog. A dog who'd earned his living the hard way, hunting wild boar and leopards.

"Go away," said Melanie, her heart beating fast. Her knees had gone funny, and she felt a little sick. Her mind kept trying to give her a reason for what she'd seen when she knew that really, there wasn't one. There was a man and a dog, three women and a pot. It sounded like the opening line of a bad joke. She took a deep breath, turned her back on him, and walked away. After a moment she heard the click-click-click of claws on concrete behind her. She walked a little faster. The clicking speeded up.

When she reached the end of the path she was back on the main road. The grounds of the museum were cut off from her by iron railings. There were no houses. Although the rain had stopped it was still cloudy, and there was no one about.

She broke into a jog, and still the dog kept up with her. And then there was a flash of lightning, followed by a huge crash of thunder. She lost her nerve, and started to run as though the hounds of hell were at her heels. Seconds later the heavens opened, and the rain lashed at her face and into her eyes. She was running down the hill now – she couldn't stop, she couldn't see. When the tree suddenly loomed up in front of her it was too late to do anything but crash into it.

"Are you OK?"

Melanie opened her eyes. She was looking at a boy of about her own age, with brown eyes, sandy hair and freckles.

"You haven't broken anything, have you?" he asked.

"Only my phone," said Melanie, sitting up. She could feel bits of plastic in her pocket, and her head hurt.

The boy glanced behind him. "Your dog found me. He came up to me, grabbed me by the sleeve, and got me to follow him. He's a bit of a star, isn't he? What's his name?"

"Sirius," said Melanie, saying the first name that came into her head. Sirius was the name the Greeks had given to the Dog Star. The brightest of all stars.

"I don't have a phone," said the boy. "If I did I would call an ambulance. You hit your head. You might have concussion."

"I'm OK," said Melanie. "Really." She just wanted to get home, curl up with a hot drink and forget about everything. She stood up.

He looked thoughtful. Then he said, "Do you want me to walk back with you? In case you feel a bit dizzy? My name's Simon, by the way."

"I'm Melanie," she said. "And yes, please." Things were quite weird enough without having to walk home alone in a strange area with a 3,000-year-old dog at her heels. On the other hand, it was the 3,000-year-old dog who had gone for help.

Simon was tall and thin, and he went to the boys' school four miles away. His mother was dead, and he lived with his father. Melanie thought about asking him in for a coffee. He didn't seem very sure what to do either. In the end they both just said goodbye.

Melanie could have kicked herself. She didn't know where Simon lived – she didn't even know his surname. He was the only friend she'd made since they'd moved here. She couldn't afford to be so careless.

"I've been followed home by a dog," Melanie told her mother, as she walked into the hall.

"Oh," said Roberta, Melanie's mum. "I hate dogs. You can't keep him."

Sirius wagged his tail, rolled onto his back with his paws in the air and looked appealing.

"Oh, all right, then," said Melanie's mother. "Just until someone claims him. I'll put an advert in the local paper. And I don't want him in the dining room, on the new carpet. Not that we're likely to get any visitors."

"I thought you used to live round here," said Melanie. "Haven't you got any old school friends or anything?"

"No."

They hadn't lived in the house for very long. Melanie's grandfather had died, and her father had been left the house and the family business, and he was away a lot. Melanie had started at her new school the week before. It was the same school her mother had attended – and she hated it. She couldn't wait for Friday, when they broke up for the summer.

"How old were you when you left school?" she asked her mother.

"What is this," said Roberta, "the Spanish Inquisition? It's a long time ago. I don't remember."

Melanie shook her head. She didn't believe it. *How could you not remember something like that?*

Chapter 3
A Face from the Past

The last day of term was hot. As Melanie left the school grounds, the woman stepped out from the behind a tree like the grim reaper, and said, "Roberta Lee's girl. Am I right?"

Lee had been Roberta's name before she got married. Melanie nodded.

"You look like her. Same eyes. As though someone's just gone ... 'boo!'"

Melanie jumped, and the woman laughed. There was the scar of an old burn or something on her neck, and she smelt of vodka.

"I'm meeting my mother," said Melanie, "I can't stop."

"Jolly good," said the woman. "I'll come with you." There were yellow nicotine stains on her fingers, and her nails were bitten all the way down. They started to walk. "What's your name?"

"Melanie." She speeded up, but the woman kept up with her quite easily.

"I'm Denise."

Melanie wondered if the woman had gone to school with Roberta. It didn't seem likely, she looked so much older.

"Good grief, you don't have very much to say for yourself, do you? I'd have thought you'd have lots of things to ask me about."

"What sort of things?"

"Well," said the woman, "I was a Jack Russell."

The woman was a complete nutter, no doubt about it.

"A *Jack Russell*," repeated Denise, as though it should mean something to Melanie.

"You were a dog in a former life?" guessed Melanie.

The woman stopped smoking, threw her fag end to the ground and trod on it. "You're hard work, aren't you? Didn't your mother ever tell you about the Jack Russells?"

Melanie shook her head. They weren't very far from the car park now – she wouldn't have to put up with this for much longer.

"We were a club, a secret society. She never told you about us?"

"No," said Melanie, beginning to get interested in spite of herself. "How many of you were there?"

"Three."

"What did you do? Solve crimes? Chase smugglers and drink gallons of lemonade?"

The woman laughed. "We had adventures beyond your wildest night-mares, Melanie."

"I don't have night-mares," said Melanie. She was thinking, *Not at night, anyway.*

"Well, lucky old you," sneered Denise.

They crossed the car park, their feet crunching over the gravel. Roberta was leaning against the car, relaxed and elegant. She spotted Melanie. Then she saw Denise, and froze.

"Hello, Robbo," said Denise.

Roberta turned as white as a sheet.

Melanie looked from Denise to her mother and back again. "You did go to school together, then?"

"Same class," said Denise.

Roberta was looking at Denise in a very strange way, checking her out bit by bit. She paused for a moment at the scar on her neck.

Denise said, "We need to talk, Robbo."

"I don't think so," replied Roberta. "And don't call me Robbo."

Denise looked at Roberta closely for a moment as though she was trying to read her. Then she said, "Don't tell me you've never heard their voices. We could be rid of them forever, now you've come back."

"They? Who's *they*?" snapped Roberta.

"You know who they are. The Kindly Ones."

Melanie felt the hairs on the back of her neck prickle. *The Kindly Ones were what the women on the vase had called themselves.*

"I don't know what you're talking about," said Roberta. She had a strange blank look on her face.

"Do you know what day it is?" said Denise.

"Friday," said Roberta.

"It's the last day of term, Robbo.
Remember the last day of term, 25 years ago?
The day they got out?"

"Come along, Melanie," said Roberta,
opening the car door.

A look of real anger crossed Denise's face.
Then she just turned and walked away. As she
vanished into the trees Sirius bounced over
and jumped into the car, damp and muddy.
Roberta looked annoyed and pushed him into
the back, but there were dark paw-prints on
the seats.

"Who were the Jack Russells?" asked
Melanie, putting her seat-belt on.

"School-girl rubbish, Melanie. Ginger beer
and ghost stories." Roberta drove out of the
car park and into the lane.

"Tell me about them," said Melanie.

"Nothing to tell. There were three of us, me, Denise and Stephanie."

"Why don't you all meet up again?"

A faint expression of horror crossed Roberta's face. "I don't think so," she said. "Stephanie might have turned out like Denise." She crashed the gears and looked annoyed.

"Did you have passwords? Codes? A secret meeting place?"

"Shall we have pizza tonight?" said Melanie's mother.

Melanie gave up.

That evening Roberta asked Melanie to take some boxes up to the attic. "It's going to take months to get the house sorted out," she said bitterly. "I never wanted to move here."

Melanie dropped the last box. It was only when she knelt down and started to tidy up

20

that she saw the photograph. It was black and white, and beginning to go yellow at the edges. Three girls, wearing striped summer dresses. One of them was her mother, plump and more cheerful. Then there was Denise, looking slim and elegant. The third girl, with freckles, must be Stephanie. *How amazing.* Melanie put the photograph in her bag.

Chapter 4
Teamwork

The following day Roberta suddenly decided to go to a fair. They'd just left the cake stall when Melanie spotted Simon. He saw her at the same time, and he waved.

"Who's that?" asked Roberta.

"No one special."

"No one special, eh?" Simon started to walk towards them. "I think I'll go and have a coffee. Meet you back here in 20 minutes," Roberta said with a sly smile. Then she walked off.

"Hi," said Melanie.

"Hi," said Simon. He seemed awkward. "You get some great bargains at the book stall here. This one's about the Greek myths. Medusa and the Furies and all that."

They visited some other stalls, and exchanged phone numbers.

"Aren't you going to introduce me?" asked Roberta, appearing from nowhere. Melanie's mother peered rather closely at Simon and said, "I don't know you, do I? You don't deliver our papers?"

Simon shook his head.

"You look very familiar," said Roberta. "Maybe I know your mother."

"My mother's been dead for 10 years," said Simon.

Roberta looked shocked. "I'm so sorry," she said. "Was it sudden?"

Melanie could have died. "I'll give you a ring, Simon," she said, and she started to walk away.

"Hang on," said Roberta, catching hold of Melanie's bag.

The strap broke, and the bag scattered its contents across the grass. As Simon bent down to help, he saw the photograph of the three Jack Russells – but just as he was about to give it back he stopped. An expression of amazement crossed his face. He looked at Melanie and said, "Where did you get this?"

"What is it?" asked Roberta.

"It's a photograph of my mother and some other people," said Simon. "When they were at school."

Roberta grabbed the photograph, and stared at it. Then she turned to face Simon and said faintly, "What was your mother's name?"

"Stephanie."

The colour drained from Roberta's face and she said, "How did she die?"

Simon looked upset. "She was ill," he said. "She heard voices. She killed herself."

****

It was a relief when Simon *did* ring the next morning. Melanie thought that her mother's behaviour the day before had been the pits.

"Fancy my mother knowing yours," he said. "What do you know about her?" There was a sort of hunger in his voice. A longing to hear something, *anything*, about his mother.

"Nothing, Simon, I'm sorry."

"Didn't your mum ever talk about her?"

"She never talked about school," said Melanie. "I've learnt more in the last few days than I ever knew before. Listen ..." She told him about Denise and the voices she heard, and the way the Jack Russells used to meet in the museum. How spooky she found the place.

Simon didn't interrupt. "Spooky indeed," he said when she'd finished. "Denise hears voices, my mother jumped out of a window to get away from *her* voices, and your mother seems to have blanked the past. I wonder what happened to them on the last day of term? We could try the library. They keep all the old local papers. We know the year, and the date's going to be round about the 20th of July."

It hadn't occurred to Melanie that they could do this properly, like detectives. What a wicked way to spend the summer holidays!

****

The library was small and old-fashioned. At long last they found a newspaper photograph of the museum, under a pall of

smoke like a dark cloud. The headline read:
Cause of Fire Still a Mystery.

"It's the right date," said Simon. "And you
say the Jack Russells used to meet there?
I wonder if there's a connection?"

Melanie wanted to tell him what had
happened to *her* in the museum, but however
she ordered the words in her head they
sounded back-to-front and stupid. They spent
the rest of the afternoon searching through
the newspapers, but they didn't find anything
further.

The rain started as they got half-way up
the hill. Simon was wearing a baggy raincoat,
and he took it off and held it over their heads.
It flapped with each gust of wind, and the rain
pattered on it the way it would on an umbrella.

The flapping was getting louder, but the
wind seemed to have dropped. It didn't make
sense. They were nearly at the top of the hill
now – they would pass the museum in a

moment. And then Melanie heard something else, something she couldn't quite place ... a hissing ...

She went cold. She could only see right in front of her – she didn't know what was either side of them, let alone what was behind them. Now she could smell burning, and if she listened really hard she could hear the soft explosions of sparks every so often, and the distant crack of a whip.

"Melanie ..." breathed the voice that was the wind echoing through an empty building. "Melanie Dunn ..."

Simon stopped. "What's the matter?" he said.

"What do you want from me?" Melanie said in a whisper.

There was a cackle of laughter, like the empty rattle of bones.

"I don't want anything from you, Melanie," said Simon. "What on earth's the matter?" He dropped the raincoat.

There were no women, nothing, just rain-drops. The voices had gone.

"Look," said Simon, "if you think I was going to try anything on under that raincoat you've got it completely wrong."

Melanie shook her head. She couldn't think of anything to say that would explain what she'd said.

Simon put his raincoat back on and they walked the rest of the way to the top of the hill in silence, and well apart. Somewhere in the back of her mind she felt insulted that 'trying something on' was so repellent to him.

Chapter 5

The Kindly Ones

"The last time the Jack Russells were together ..." began Melanie.

Roberta looked annoyed and snapped, "Don't start all that again." Then she changed, and said, "Look, finding out about Stephanie ... It's been a shock. If I tell you about that day, will you stop asking me? It was the last day of term. It was really hot, and we tied our jumpers round our waists as we walked up Hangman's Hill. We were going to have our final meeting."

"In the museum?"

"No, in the vault ..."

"What's a vault?"

"A sort of under-ground store room. It was in the back garden. There was a hole in the railings – we could get in any time. We used to keep biscuits down there, bottles of lemonade, notebooks ... Anyway, we were going to swear to meet again, in 25 years' time."

"Did you swear on anything?"

Roberta laughed. "Yes. Denise wanted us to swear on something old, one of the pots, to make us keep our word. She broke into the cabinet with a pen-knife. When she lifted the vase out we could see that it had been broken before, and mended. We all stood there, looking at the picture ... a man with a dog ... just like your Sirius. Then we put our hands on the pot, and the next thing I remember is sitting at the sewing machine, nearly a year later. I've no idea what happened."

"Didn't you ask anyone?"

"Like who? That year my mother died, and I don't remember a thing about it. They said it was the shock of her death that triggered the memory loss. Stephanie had gone away to America, and I'd lost touch with Denise. Let's change the subject. Are you going to see any more of Simon this summer?"

Oh no, thought Melanie, *I know what you're thinking and it isn't like that at all … what do I say?* And then she thought, *Don't say anything. Let her think he's my boyfriend. It makes it so much easier to carry on playing detective.*

****

The next day Melanie met Simon in the park.

"Right," she said. "I want you to listen to what I have to say, and then I want you to tell me that I'm not going mental. I've heard the voices as well."

For a moment, Simon didn't respond. Then he said, "Go on."

Melanie told him everything, from the moment she'd heard the tapping inside the display case to what Roberta had told her about that last day of term. He didn't interrupt.

When she'd finished, he said, "I think we'd better go and see Denise."

"You don't think I'm a nutcase, then?"

Simon glanced at the dog. "He's real enough."

"I don't know where Denise lives," said Melanie.

"I do," said Simon. "Next door to the pub."

The side passage to Denise's back garden was blocked by a dustbin, full of empty bottles.

33

The path to the front door was overgrown with weeds and the doorbell didn't work. Simon banged on the door with his fist.

When Denise opened the door she just stood there, staring at the dog.

"Can we talk to you?" asked Melanie.

"You can try," said Denise.

They followed her into the sitting room. She pointed to the sofa, and as they sat down there was a cloud of dust and an angry creak.

"I can't offer you a coffee," said Denise. "I haven't got enough cups. And come to think of it I haven't got any coffee either." She looked at Simon. "Who are you? Melanie's boyfriend?"

"No," said Simon quickly. "Stephanie was my mother."

Denise drew her breath in sharply. Then she said, "That dog. How long have you had him?"

34

Melanie bit her lip. "Since I broke the vase."

Denise froze. "He *is* the dog on the vase, then? And the ... you know. *Them*. The Kindly Ones. Did they ...?"

"Yes. They got out as well."

Denise groaned. "I should have expected it. It'll be 25 years next week. Just the sort of trick they'd pull. Nothing was fair in Ancient Greece. Children were punished for the sins of their parents ..."

Simon fiddled with his watch, but didn't say anything.

"I should never have gone back to the museum," said Denise. "Should have known better, with a degree in archaeology, the study of really old buildings. And objects. Such as pots."

"I know what archaeology is," said Simon, with a smile.

35

"I even earned my living at it, once upon a time." She laughed. "They were waiting for me, after Stephanie's funeral. That's why I drink. To forget."

Oh, wow, thought Melanie, *it's such a relief to be talking about all this openly, without worrying about how crazy I sound.*

"The thing about the Furies ..." said Denise. "Whoops. Mustn't call them that. It's bad Karma. Call them the Kindly Ones, and they might give you a miss one night. They drive their victims mad, you see. By making them do terrible things to themselves."

"What sort of things?" asked Simon.

Denise put her hand to the scar on her neck. "They told me I could get away from them by hanging myself. You don't tie very good knots when you're drunk, though, and I ended up in hospital instead."

"My mother jumped out of a window," said Simon.

Nobody spoke for a while.

"Medicine time," said Denise, reaching for a vodka bottle. "Off you go."

Simon and Melanie looked at one another.

"Go on, get out," shouted Denise, suddenly furious. "You let them get out again, you idiot, after everything I did. You let them *loose*."

Simon and Melanie went.

Chapter 6

Under the Museum

When they got to the top of Hangman's Hill, Simon said, "I'm going into the museum."

Melanie stared at him. *"What?"*

"I want to see for myself."

"I thought you believed me."

"Be fair. Denise gets drunk enough to see the Taj Mahal out of the sitting room window."

"I see," said Melanie coldly.

"I just want to see for myself," repeated Simon.

"Well, I'm not coming in with you."

"Fair enough," said Simon, and he walked off down the path to the museum.

Melanie just stood there, feeling let down. After a while she heard the door creak open, and close again. And then, as if someone had whistled for him, Sirius dashed through the gate and vanished between the yew trees. Annoyed, Melanie followed him round the side of the building, and into the back garden. She spotted him in some nettles, digging at something with his paws. He turned to look at her, and barked. She went over. Between the nettles was a piece of rusty corrugated iron, so she kicked it to one side. There were stone steps beneath it, going down into darkness.

The vault!

Had the Jack Russells left anything down there, in their meeting place? Scratched their names on the wall? Although she knew it was a bad idea – no one knew where she was, for one thing – Melanie felt she just had to go in. She desperately wanted to know more about the year her mother couldn't remember. There might just be some sort of clue. She switched on her key-ring torch, took a deep breath, and went down the steps. Sirius didn't follow her. At the bottom was a wooden door. She pushed it, and, to her surprise, it swung open.

The vault itself was made of bricks. It was much bigger than she thought it would be. It was about half the size of a tennis court. The roof was arched, and there were black iron rings set in the wall at head-level. The floor had been paved with stone and the whole effect was cool and musty. Melanie left the door wide open, and went inside.

At the far end there was a shelf set back into the wall in a small alcove. She shone the narrow beam of her torch into the opening. And there it was. A wooden box. She wiped the dust off it, and underneath she saw, written in black paint: *Property of the Jack Russells. Keep out.* With her heart pounding Melanie levered up the rusty catch until it broke, and lifted the lid. She reached inside and pulled out a packet of biscuits, which collapsed between her fingers as the contents crumbled to dust. The only other thing in there was a metal badge with the word *Prefect* written on it.

Feeling very disappointed, she put the badge in her pocket, stood up, and turned back towards the entrance. For a moment she felt confused. Then she realised what had happened. The door had swung shut. She walked over to it, but this time it wouldn't open. It wouldn't budge at all. She twisted and pulled and tugged at the metal ring – nothing. She stopped for a moment and listened. Was Sirius still out there? "Sirius?" she called. But there was no bark for an answer. What she heard instead was distant, echoey laughter. An icy draught like a small wind sprang up from nowhere, and she shivered. And then the battery in her torch ran out and she was in the dark.

The Kindly Ones have trapped you here, said a voice inside her head. *You'll never get out. They've been very clever. No flapping cloaks this time, no smoky torches, no hissing snakes ... just your own voice in your head. Why don't you go down the steps, Melanie? It'll be all right ...*

She shouted a few times, hoping the sound would carry. Then she hammered on the door with her fists, shouted, screamed, kicked it, kicked it again. After that she slid down the wall until she was sitting with her back against the bare brick, and cried. It didn't altogether blot out the laughter, so faint it was hardly there, and it didn't stop the awful cold that was chilling her to the bone.

She must have fallen asleep, for suddenly she was aware that it was a lot later and she couldn't feel her fingers because they were so cold. She was going to freeze to death, but she was so cold she didn't mind. She just needed to doze off again ... *If only that annoying sound would go away.* It was like the sound of dragging feet ...

There was a sudden flood of light as the door opened. She shaded her eyes with her hand and stood up.

"Are you in there?" called an elderly male voice.

The flash-light shifted to one side and she saw the museum attendant. She blinked at him. He looked rumpled and he needed a shave, as though somebody had got him out of bed. Sirius was standing there behind him, his tail waving back and forth. She knelt down and hugged him.

"Come on, lass," said the attendant. "Your mother's outside waiting for you."

She followed him up the steps, and no whips cracked, and nobody laughed. And then they were outside in the warm, and Roberta was waiting for her on the path with a face like thunder.

"What happened?" asked Melanie. "Did Sirius lead you to me?"

Roberta glanced at the dog, tight-lipped. "I was out of my mind with worry by the time he showed up. Rang everyone I could think of."

"Did you phone Simon?"

"Of course I phoned Simon. Eleven times, if you must know. No reply."

Chapter 7

Attack

The following day Roberta was still furious, so Melanie decided to pay Simon a visit. Although they'd parted on bad terms, they hadn't been *that* bad.

His father opened the door. He hadn't shaved and he looked as though he had other things on his mind. He seemed surprised to see her. "Who are you?" he demanded.

"Melanie Dunn."

"I didn't think Simon knew any girls." He looked her up and down. Then he said, "Well,

well. That might explain a lot. Simon's in hospital."

Melanie heard herself say, "Has he had an accident?"

"I suppose you could call it that. Tried to kill himself. Cut his wrists. Found him at three o'clock this morning." He was looking at her as though this was her fault.

"Is he all right?"

"He'll live."

"He seemed OK when I last saw him," said Melanie faintly. "About five o'clock."

"Did he?"

"What has he said?" Melanie asked.

"Nothing," replied Simon's father.

"Can I visit him?"

"Do you really think that's a good idea?"

"Mr Brown," said Melanie, "I really would like to know why you think it's got something to do with me."

"You young girls," said Simon's father. "You don't think, do you? You lead them on, then you pack them in. That's what happened, isn't it?"

"No, it isn't," said Melanie. "We're just friends."

Mr Brown laughed. "A likely story," he said. "No, I don't want you visiting him." And he slammed the door in her face.

Melanie felt sick. *She'd* got Simon into all this, it was *her* fault that the Kindly Ones had attacked him. Because that had to be what had happened.

She would have to go and see Denise again.

Denise opened the door wearing something vile round her neck in green and orange. On a closer look it appeared to be a necklace, with large beads in the shape of limes and tangerines.

"On your own?" said Denise. "No Simon? No backbone, men. Useless."

"Can I come in?" asked Melanie.

Denise gave a shrug, and led the way into the sitting room.

Melanie told her all about what had happened in the vault, and Simon's accident.

"He'll be safe in hospital," said Denise, fiddling with her necklace and using the fruit like worry beads. "They'll watch people who've tried to kill themselves very carefully. You have to get the Furies back inside the pot, Melanie, and mend it properly. Oh, God, there I go, using their name again."

Melanie took a deep breath. "I need to know what happened, all those years ago."

Denise nodded, and reached for the vodka bottle. "The fire – that's when they got out. We were in the museum, all three of us, Stephanie, Roberta and me ..."

Melanie felt another piece of the jigsaw slide into place. "You were there?" she said. "You were in the museum on the day of the fire?"

Denise looked at Melanie. "I thought you knew."

"Knew what?"

"That Stephanie's mother died in the fire. That's why they haunted us like ghosts, only worse. Much worse. Because they blamed Stephanie for her death."

This was a real shock.

Melanie tried to swallow, but her mouth had gone far too dry. "But why did they haunt all of you?" she croaked. "Why not just Stephanie?"

49

"Fair play didn't exist in Ancient Greece."

"You said the Furies ..."

"Stop calling them that."

"You said we have to get those ... women ... back inside the pot. But how on earth do we do it?"

"You need a crash course in mending old pottery. I'm not going to touch the thing, not until I have to. It'll need all three Jack Russells to seal it forever."

"But Stephanie's dead, and there's no way my mother would get involved in any of this."

"Simon will do. They'll take the sons and the daughters if they can't get the parents."

"So I could represent Roberta."

"Yes."

"So that does make three of us. You, me and Simon. When shall we do it?"

Denise poured herself a drink, and gulped it down in one go. Then she fiddled with her necklace and said, "You really didn't know about the fire, when we went into the museum for our last meeting? When we swore to meet again, in 25 years' time? Stephanie said the first of August was the best date."

"Why?"

"She read the tea-leaves. She was into that sort of thing, despite being the only one of us who was goody-goody enough to be a prefect and get one of those metal badges."

Melanie took the badge out of her pocket.

"Yep," said Denise. "That was hers. We'd just got our hands on the pot to swear we'd meet again when her mother burst in. She was a bit odd, Stephanie's mother."

"Odd?"

"All right, she wasn't odd, she was completely mental. Used to disappear for months on end when she had another spell in the loony bin. She yelled at Stephanie. She accused her of trying to steal the pot. Grabbed a sword off the wall, and knocked it against some electric cables. That's what started the fire. The vase cracked in the heat, and the Kindly Ones got out. They started to haunt Stephanie, blaming her for her mother's death, and fifteen years later she couldn't take it any longer and killed herself.

After that they started on me instead. I was working as an archaeologist by then, so I thought I would try and fix the pot myself. The things that had been damaged in the fire were kept in the cellar. No one knew what was broken and what just needed cleaning. What I didn't realise was that the repair wouldn't last very long unless it was done by all three Jack Russells."

"It's the first of August on Thursday," said Melanie.

"Is it?" said Denise. "Good-oh. The Kindly Ones prefer superstition to fair play. They like things to be done the old way. Come round tomorrow for a pottery-repair lesson."

Chapter 8
A Pottery Lesson

On the way back from Denise's, Melanie rang the hospital. Simon had been sent home, but there was no reply when she phoned him. For once, though, luck was on her side. Simon had sneaked out to the corner shop, and she bumped into him as he came out. He had bandages on his wrists, and she was shocked to see how pale and washed-out he looked.

"I'm not meant to leave the house," he said, "but my dad had to go back to the office, so I nipped out for some chocolate. He'll be away for a couple of hours – why don't you come back to my place? It's not far."

Simon's house was nothing like Melanie's. There were books everywhere. On the hall floor, in the bathroom, even on top of the fridge. Nothing matched, either. The wallpaper was a different colour from the curtains, the curtains were a different shade from the carpet, and the carpet was a different green from the sofa.

Melanie followed Simon upstairs to his room. They both sat on the floor, and Simon drew his knees up in front of him. "I must have been walking in my sleep," he said. "I do that, sometimes. Anyway, I found myself in the bathroom, and I heard ... laughter. Sort of scary, echoey, weird. Then I saw them, in the mirror. The snakes, the whips, the long black hair. The torch-light was flickering on the white tiles. 'You can't escape us, Simon,' they hissed. 'The Furies will follow you everywhere. You will have no peace. You'll end up like your mother, locked away in a madhouse. We shall visit you each night, bringing you dreams of burning flesh, and you'll wake up screaming, night after night, until you dare not fall asleep ...' So I picked up the bathroom scales, and smashed the mirror."

"Blimey," said Melanie.

"Glass everywhere. 'Pick a piece up,' they said, 'and feel the edge.' So I did. I ran my thumb along it. And it felt wonderful, cold and sharp. Then they told me there was only one way out. I knew what they meant – so I did it. Both wrists, and I didn't feel a thing. There was a lot of blood, though. I must have fainted, because I knocked over all the bottles of shampoo and stuff. And that's what woke my dad."

"That's so scary," said Melanie. "That they could make you do that. I've got something to tell you, too ... And something to give you."

She handed over the prefect's badge. "This was your mother's."

"Wow," said Simon, his face lighting up. "I never knew she was a prefect."

So then Melanie told him about going to see Denise, and, as tactfully as she could, she told him how Stephanie's mother had died. Stephanie's mother had, after all, been his grandmother.

He took it well. Then he went over to his bookcase, pulled out a paperback, and passed it to Melanie. She read the entry about the Furies. About how they punished those who committed crimes against mothers. How they didn't just punish them, but also their grand-children and their great-grand-children, on and on. How they drove people insane.
"I think that vase is a gate-way between their world and ours," he said. "Destroying the pot could keep them here forever. It has to be mended. Sealed. With everything that was

meant to be there back inside. Including the dog."

****

"I'm really angry with you," said Roberta, when Melanie got home. "Fancy leaving the back door open."

"It was so that Sirius could get in and out," said Melanie.

"Oh, he went out all right," snarled Roberta. "He's gone. Vanished."

Melanie felt herself go cold. "He can't have. The back gate was bolted."

"He must have jumped over the wall, then."

"But ..."

"Dogs can jump, you know, Melanie."

"I'm going out to look for him," said Melanie.

But she didn't find him. That night, she cried herself to sleep.

****

On their way to Denise's house the next day, Melanie and Simon pinned *Lost Dog* posters to all the trees.

When they arrived, they were surprised at how organised Denise had suddenly become. She had broken a cheap vase, and laid the pieces out on a sheet of newspaper. Next to them stood a collection of bottles and tubes, as well as some brown tape and tweezers, and a big lump of plasticine. She told them to wash their hands. Then she began to teach them how to put a vase back together. How to support the pieces with plasticene. How to put them back in the right order. When they completed the job she broke it once more and made them start all over again.

By the end of the afternoon they were quite good at it. "You have to plan how you do it very carefully," Denise explained, "or a piece could get 'locked out'. It won't fit in the gap left. And then you'd have to break it and begin again."

"Oh, I see," said Simon. "The problem's that when the *inside* of one piece is wider than the *outside* it won't fit. It doesn't matter until you get to the very last bit because it has to go underneath the edges of the pieces on either side."

"Very good," said Denise. "Puzzles are clearly your thing."

"Denise," said Melanie, "does everything that was painted on the pot really have to go back inside?"

"Yes."

"We've got a problem, then. The dog, Sirius."

"What about him?"

"He's vanished."

Denise groaned, and reached for the vodka bottle. "It'll only be a short-term fix again, then. It won't last."

****

When Melanie got home, Roberta's face told her that there was no news. Melanie picked at her dinner, and went to bed early. She wasn't looking forward to the next day one little bit. But she lay awake for hours. An icy fear built up inside her. She heard the sound of whips in her head, and saw burnt bodies and slashed wrists. She tossed and turned for ages, until in the end the thoughts drifted, muddied and faded, and she fell asleep.

Chapter 9
The Furies' Revenge

When Melanie arrived at the museum, Simon was already there. He gave her a faint smile and said, "No Sirius, then?"

"No."

"No Denise, either. Just a short-term fix, then, like the one she did last time."

"Better than nothing, I suppose," said Melanie.

They waited for what seemed like a long time, but neither Denise nor Sirius showed. In the end Simon looked at Melanie. Melanie nodded, and they opened the door and stepped into the gloom.

They could hear the museum attendant in his office. He was listening to a cricket match on his radio. It sounded tinny and distant. But when they arrived at the cabinet the vase wasn't in three pieces any more. The three pieces of the pot had become seven.

"That must have been me," said Simon. "Good job the attendant doesn't do his job properly."

"He's really old," said Melanie. She had to force herself to open the cabinet and lift out the pieces. The room had gone icy cold, and she could see her own breath like little puffs of smoke. They went down the steps to the cellar, where they wouldn't be disturbed. Both of them were wondering if they were really up to the task.

The room was lit by one light bulb. There was a workbench against the wall. Simon emptied the contents of his back-pack on it. There were little bottles of chemicals, a roll of tape, blades, spatulas, a packet of plasticine, and a small lamp. There was no electric socket in the cellar so he had brought an extension cable. He attached the cable to the lamp, gave the other end to Melanie and said, "See if you can find a socket somewhere upstairs."

Melanie looped the cable over her arm and went back up the steps. She found a socket over by the window, plugged in the cable, and switched it on.

She could have sworn she'd left the cellar door ajar. As she fiddled with the latch she heard a faint burst of applause from the radio, hands clapping and voices cheering. And then the crack of someone hitting a ball. At least, it *sounded* like someone hitting a cricket ball ... or cracking a whip ...

"Melanie ..." It was the sound of the wind echoing through an empty building.

Ignore it. Just open the door.

"Melanie ... We won't go back in the pot."

The latch moved a little, but not enough.

"We like it here."

And suddenly the speaker was right there beside her, red eyes, chalk-white skin, long black hair. She reached out her hand, and closed it over Melanie's. Her touch burnt like fire. Or ice. See-through crystals formed on Melanie's wrist, tinkling as they fell away, showering the floor with frost. She staggered back, and the second woman appeared in a cloud of smoke. The third stepped out shadow-like from behind her, snakes writhing like living bracelets round her arms. The Furies' faces were twisted with hatred. And, savage as they were, they were beautiful too.

The first one trailed the whip across the palm of her hand. Then she raised it, and Melanie heard the whistle of the whip's lash as it came down across her face. Her head snapped back, and her eyes watered. She screamed, but no sound came out.

The woman lifted the whip to her lips, licked the blood from it, seized Melanie by the hair and pushed her to her knees. "We will have you," she hissed, "body and soul. We will have you for ever." She moved the torch closer and the ends of Melanie's hair caught fire, frizzled, then flaked away like ash. She could feel something wet on her face, but she didn't know if it was tears or blood.

The woman jerked Melanie's head, and a handful of hair came away in her fist. She fingered it. Then she started to eat it. The others growled and tried to snatch some, and for a moment the three Furies fought and scrapped like animals. Then the hair was gone, and they were licking their lips and looking at her. It could have been Africa, and they could have been a pack of hyenas looking at a zebra.

They moved in again, slowly, with sure and certain steps, their arms held out towards her. She tried to focus, saw the flicker of a snake's tongue, close, too close to her face. As she turned her head to avoid it she felt it slither round her neck, cool and like leather. And then the snake began to tighten, it was getting difficult to breathe, and still she couldn't move ... or was it her own hands around her neck ... she couldn't be sure ... there were little sparks of light everywhere, and the sound of roaring in her ears ...

Far away a door banged, and a moment later something white flashed past. The snake uncoiled itself and let go, and the Furies backed away. At last Melanie could breathe again. Sirius stood there, stiff-legged, growling.

Chapter 10
A Race Against Time

"They're here!" cried Melanie, running down the cellar steps with Sirius at her heels. "All three of them!"

"Good," said Simon.

He had supported two of the fragments of the pot with lumps of plasticine. He had glued them together, and held them in place with tape. Melanie could see part of the rim of the vase, the thick edge like the body of a snake. She almost expected to see guts spilling out of the broken bit, and tiny bones poking through.

Instead the edges were clean and solid, like a broken lump of chocolate.

"I've washed everything in alcohol," said Simon. "I'm trying to get two halves of the pot completed, so we can use them like a trap."

Melanie put her hand to her face. There was no cut, no blood, nothing. *But it felt so real*, she thought. *The pain, the snake around my neck, was it all in my mind?*

Simon taped another piece into place, but this one didn't seem to fit properly. "It's sprung," he said. "Gone flat. Lost its curve. It needs the piece on the other side to hold it in position. This is going to have to be fast work."

As he glued a piece of the second half into place, Melanie smelt smoke. She glanced up. One of the Furies was standing at the top of the steps, with murder in her eyes. The others were right behind her.

Simon had two mended halves of the pot on the bench now. They were opposite one another, ready.

"Simon," purred the woman, "take off your bandage. The wound itches, doesn't it? Take out the safety-pin and scratch it, Simon, scratch it through to the bone ..."

Simon rubbed his wrist against the bench.

"Don't listen to her," shouted Melanie desperately.

Simon was beginning to fumble, make a mess of things. Melanie could see him trying to paint the edges of the two halves with glue, but his hand was shaking. Suddenly he ripped off one of his bandages in an irritated sort of way, and went for the fresh scar with the safety-pin.

Sirius took two steps towards the woman, and snarled. She dropped her whip and covered her throat with her hands.

The snarl seemed to bring Simon to his senses. He looked at the drops of blood welling out of his wrist in horror. Then he picked up the bandage and wound it round his arm again.

The woman was backing away from Sirius now, and with every step she got closer and closer to the vase. Simon had the two pieces almost touching. The woman was moaning and weeping tears of blood. And then, suddenly, she wasn't there any more. She was back on the surface of the pot, and she was scrabbling at the glaze with her hands, like someone trapped behind a plate-glass window.

A whip snaked round Melanie's ankle, and a voice hissed, "Let my sister go. Break the pot again."

Melanie prised off the lash. It was like picking a scab.

"Smash it," the voice went on. "Or I shall rip you apart. Your mother helped Stephanie kill *her* mother. You'd do the same to your mother, given half a chance ..."

"No, I wouldn't," said Melanie. "She's only difficult to get on with because of *you*. We *do* love each other."

The woman flinched as though she'd been hit, and her torch spluttered and went out. And suddenly she'd joined the other woman on the pot.

"My mother may be dead," said Simon, between gritted teeth, "but I still love her."

The third woman howled with anger, and spat at him. She missed, and the spit sizzled on the ground like a gob of hot black tar. And then she too was pulled back into the pot. Simon pressed the two halves together.

Sirius gave Melanie a long look, full of meaning, and she felt her eyes fill with tears. Then he leapt up onto the bench, growing smaller and smaller until he could wriggle through the crack. He had only been a visitor to this world, really. His real life was elsewhere, chasing painted leopards and wild boar.

And then, with a clap like thunder, the door to the cellar flew open.

"Just in time, I see," said Denise. "That damn dog spent the whole night at my place, trying to make me to do the right thing with his big sad eyes. All hands on the pot, then."

Melanie could have hugged her. Instead, she put her hands on the vase, and Simon and Denise did the same. To begin with it felt smooth and cold, like stone. Then it started to warm through until it felt like skin, not clay – living skin with a body beneath it.

The Furies screamed in silence and writhed on the pot's surface, and they carried on writhing until the glue was hard. And then, quite suddenly, they were gone.

The only figures left on the vase were a man and a dog – both in exactly the same positions they'd been in when Melanie saw the pot that very first time.

The dark mood in the cellar suddenly lifted. The three of them grinned at one another. Melanie looked closely at Simon's face for a moment. His dark eyes, his freckles, his pale skin. He didn't look well, and there was fresh blood on one of the bandages. They made their way back up the steps, and she put the pot back in its display case.

"Now that all that's over," said Simon to Melanie, "do you still want to meet up?"

"Of course I do," she said, and on an impulse she kissed him on the cheek. His smile widened. Maybe her mother's view of their relationship wasn't so far out after all. She could hear the cricket on the radio in the background. It seemed so ordinary, pointless. Something from another world.

As they walked into the sun-light Denise took out her flask, and poured the contents onto the ground. "My liver's in for a shock," she told them, "but what the hell. Let's go and tell your mother."

Melanie smiled.

The Jack Russells would have their get-together after all, both the new members and the old, and it was going to be brilliant.

Barrington Stoke would like to thank all its readers for commenting on the manuscript before publication and in particular:

D. Allan
Alison Ball
Samantha Bernard
Jack Comaie
Gillian Ferris
Claire Graham
Bethany Lorimer
Daniel McAllister
Stephen McKerchar
Sean Mooney
Patrick John Mullins
Rachael O'Hare
Kieran Parker
Lucie Pattullo
Jordan Pedersen
Penny Ward

Become a Consultant!

Would you like to give us feedback on our titles before they are published? Contact us at the email address below – we'd love to hear from you!

info@barringtonstoke.co.uk
www.barringtonstoke.co.uk

Great reads – no problem!

Barrington Stoke books are:

Great stories – from thrillers to comedy to horror, and all by the best writers around!

No hassle – fast reads with no boring bits, and a story that doesn't let go of you till the last page.

Short – the perfect size for a fast, fun read.

We use our own font and paper to make it easier to read our books. And we ask teenagers like you, who want a no-hassle read, to check every book before it's published.

That way, we know for sure that every Barrington Stoke book is a great read for everyone.

Check out www.barringtonstoke.co.uk for more info about Barrington Stoke and our books!

If you liked this book,
why don't you try ...

Ghosting

by Keith Gray

Nat and his sister help the living contact the dead. But this time the dead are talking back. And now the screams won't stop ...

Someone should have told them there are worse things than ghosts ...

You can order *Ghosting* directly from our website at
www.barringtonstoke.co.uk

If you liked this book, why don't you try ...

Grave Dirt

by E.E. Richardson

Dirt is death ... blood is life.

Luke is dead. And Darren never got to say good-bye. He wants his best friend back and he doesn't care how he does it.

But Darren raises an evil worse than he could ever dream of – and now it's coming after him. Can he fight the monster that he's called from the grave?

You can order *Grave Dirt* directly from our website at
www.barringtonstoke.co.uk

If you liked this book,
why don't you try ...

Night Hunger

by Alan Gibbons

Ever since strange, sexy Beth sank her teeth into him, John's been feeling ... hungry. He craves meat, most of all at night. His hunger's leading him to a dark place, but can he stop himself, before it's too late?